KU-150-870

WITHDRAWN FROM STOCK

CONTENTS

I 91150 12/7 I.E.S.

ANCIENT LEGENDS OF IRELAND

SOINBHE LALLY

ILLUSTRATED BY

FINBARR O'CONNOR

POOLBEG

Leabharlann Contae na Midhe
02465921

The Coming of the Dé Danaan

The Dé Danaan were gods of beauty and light. They lived in the four cities of the sky. These were the cities of knowledge, of music, of poetry and of crafts. With their wisdom and knowledge they shaped the world.

On the first day of May they came to Ireland, sailing their golden ships high on the clouds. They found in Ireland a people called the Firbolgs and challenged them to battle. They overcame the Firbolgs and took possession of Ireland.

Nuada, King of the Dé Danaan, had his hand cut off in the battle. His physician made him a hand of silver which was perfect in every way, but his people demanded a new king. They chose a king who was handsome and young. His name was Bres.

They soon regretted their choice. Bres was mean. People who came to his castle went away hungry. He demanded heavy taxes and hoarded his wealth.

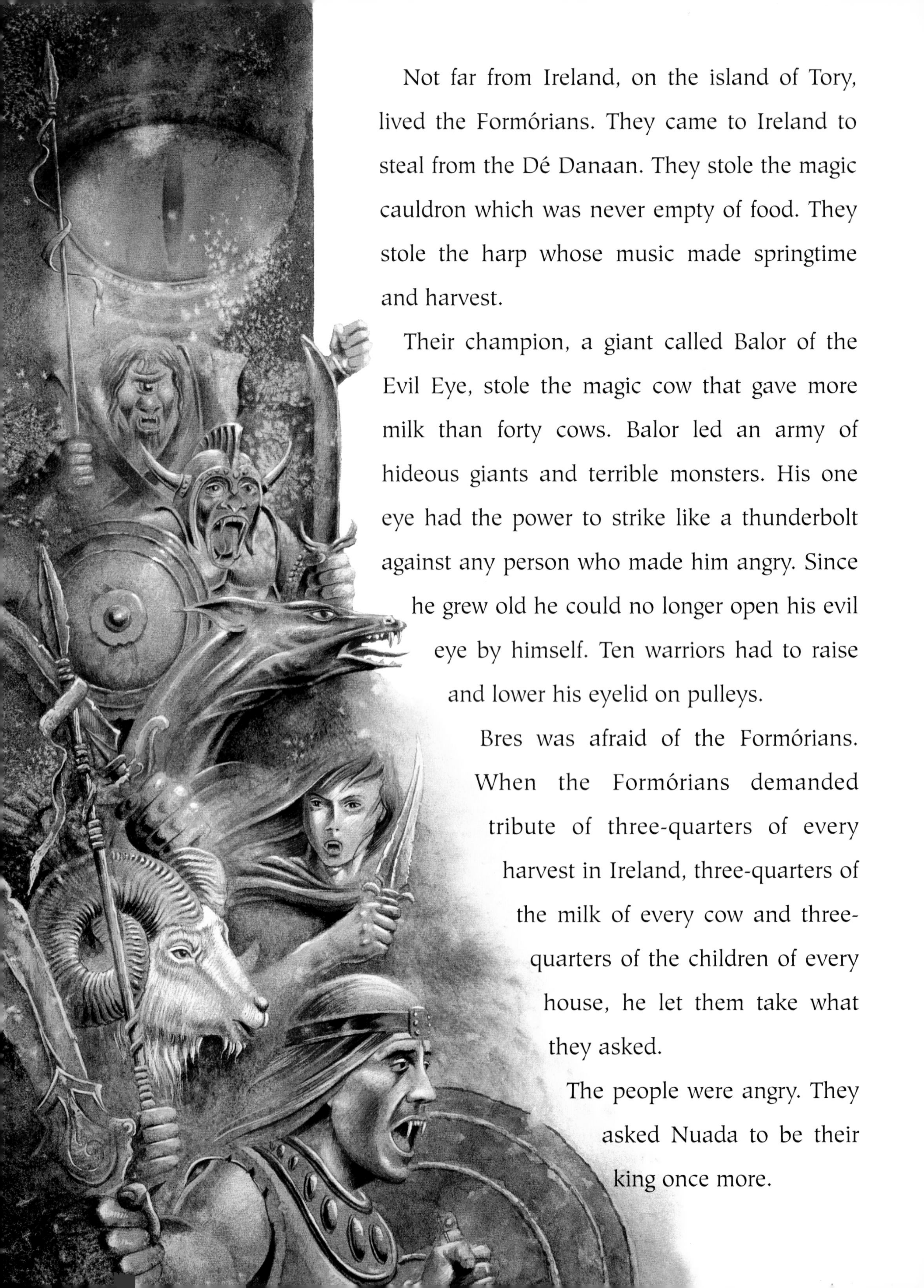

Not far from Ireland, on the island of Tory, lived the Formórians. They came to Ireland to steal from the Dé Danaan. They stole the magic cauldron which was never empty of food. They stole the harp whose music made springtime and harvest.

Their champion, a giant called Balor of the Evil Eye, stole the magic cow that gave more milk than forty cows. Balor led an army of hideous giants and terrible monsters. His one eye had the power to strike like a thunderbolt against any person who made him angry. Since he grew old he could no longer open his evil eye by himself. Ten warriors had to raise and lower his eyelid on pulleys.

Bres was afraid of the Formórians. When the Formórians demanded tribute of three-quarters of every harvest in Ireland, three-quarters of the milk of every cow and three-quarters of the children of every house, he let them take what they asked.

The people were angry. They asked Nuada to be their king once more.

Nuada of the Silver Hand prepared to wage war on the Formórians but his warriors had little heart for battle. "We need a champion to lead us," they said.

Deep in the sea, a young hero heard their call. His name was Lugh, son of a Dé Danaan warrior. When he was an infant, Manannán, god of the sea, took him as his son to live in his kingdom under the waves. Now it was time for Lugh to go back to his own people.

He rode up out of the sea on a white horse. His face shone bright as the sun and in his hand he carried the Sword of Light. "Who will help me fight against Balor?" he asked.

The rivers of Ireland spoke with one voice. "We will help you. We will rise into flood when the warriors of Formór try to cross over."

"We will crowd together and block their way," said the twelve hills of Ireland.

"We will fight at your side," said the warriors of the Dé Danaan, for the sight of Lugh filled them with courage.

The two armies met in battle. All day long they fought. As Balor struck down hundreds of Dé Danaan warriors with a look from his evil eye, hundreds more took their place.

Lugh waited until Balor grew tired and let his eyelid droop. Then, before the Formórian warriors could raise it, he drove with his sword and killed Balor with a single blow.

The Formórians fled from the battle and left the Dé Danaan to rule Ireland in peace.

Etain and Midir

Midir was a king of the Dé Danaan. He lived in a fairy dún with his wife, Fuamnach.

One day, as he crossed a stream, he saw a maiden preparing to wash her hair. Sunlight fell on the long braids as she loosened them, making her hair shine like gold. Her eyes were blue and her lips red as rowanberries.

"What is your name?" Midir asked.

"Etain."

They fell in love. Midir forgot Fuamnach and took Etain to be his wife. Fuamnach was angry and jealous. She went to a druid and asked for a spell to drive Etain away. The druid gave her the power of enchantment and she turned Etain into a butterfly. Then she raised a storm which blew the butterfly far away.

Midir was heartbroken. He searched Ireland for Etain but could not find her.

For three years the butterfly was tossed by wind and dashed by cold rains. Her days and nights were passed in misery. Then one day she flew into the castle of the high king who ruled over the mortal beings of Ireland.

The king and queen were feasting. The butterfly tried to cling to the ceiling of the great hall but fainted with weariness and dropped into the queen's goblet of wine. When the queen drank from the goblet she swallowed the butterfly.

After a time, the queen gave birth to a baby girl and named her Etain. The child grew up beautiful, with hair that shone like gold in the sun, with blue eyes and lips as red as rowanberries.

The old high king died and a young king took his place. He fell in love with Etain and they were married.

Year after year Midir went on searching for Etain. At last he found her, walking in the garden of the high king's castle. He called her name. She looked at Midir but he was a stranger to her. He realised she had forgotten her past life and went away sadly.

That night Etain dreamed of the fairy dún. She remembered her love for Midir but knew she must stay with her mortal husband.

In a few days Midir came again. He went to the king and challenged him to a game of chess. The king was eager to play with the noble stranger.

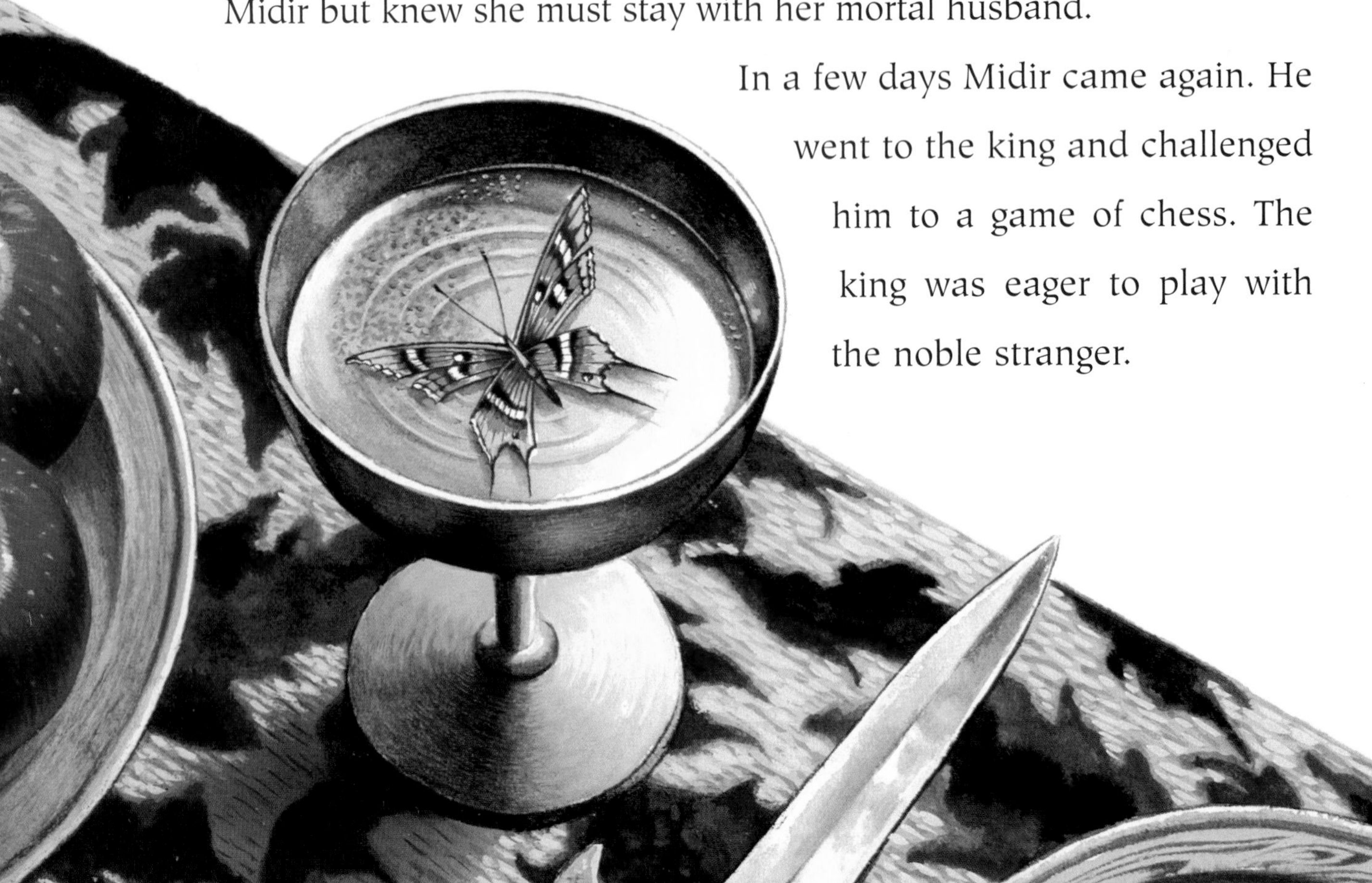

"What will be the prize?"

"Whatever the winner asks."

"Do not play," Etain said to the king because it was her duty to warn her husband, but he did not heed her.

The king and Midir played on a silver chessboard. The king won the first game. "For my prize I demand fifty horses," he said. Immediately fifty fairy horses appeared outside his castle.

They played again and the king won a second time. "For my prize I demand a forest fully grown," he said. At once a forest grew up around his castle.

They played a third time. This time Midir won. "For my prize I will take one kiss from Etain."

The king was afraid. He realised that Midir would try to take Etain away. "The queen is sleeping. Come back in a month. You may kiss her then," he said.

Midir agreed.

The king set builders to build high walls around his castle. He put three hundred of his best warriors to guard it but he knew that fairy magic was stronger than warriors or walls.

On the day that Midir was to return, the king waited in his great hall.

He kept Etain close by his side so that she could not be taken without his knowledge.

Just before noon Midir appeared in the middle of the hall. Before the king or his warriors could draw their swords, Midir took Etain in his arms and said, "I claim my kiss."

He kissed her on the lips. Together they flew up into the air and disappeared. The warriors rushed outside. They saw two swans, linked together with a golden chain, flying high above the castle. Three times the swans circled the castle and then they flew away.

Deirdre of the Sorrows

When Conor was King of Ulster a baby girl was born to the wife of his bard, Feilmidh. Cathbad the druid came to Feilmidh's house. He took the child in his arms and looked into her future.

"Your beauty will be like a flame. For your sake blood will be shed in Ulster. You will be known as Deirdre of the Sorrows and your story will be told for ever."

Feilmidh hid his daughter away. On a distant mountainside he built a small house covered with sods of grass and planted willows round it.

He asked the wise woman, Leorcham, to take the child there.

Deirdre grew up graceful and beautiful. Leorcham taught her the names of trees and flowers and birds. They were happy in their secret home.

One evening, a hunter stopped to rest near the house. He heard voices and called out for someone to let him in.

"What is that sound?" Deirdre asked and before Leorcham could stop her, she opened the door.

When the hunter saw Deirdre he said, "If the sons of Usna knew of your beauty, they would come to seek you."

"Who are the sons of Usna?"

"Naoise and his brothers. Their hair is dark and their lips are red. Naoise is the tallest and handsomest of the three."

"Be quiet," Leorcham said.

"Last night, in my dreams, I saw those three young men," Deirdre said.

Next morning the hunter went to the king and told him of Deirdre's beauty and of the place where she lived. Conor went to the place.

"Open the door for the King of Ulster," he called out and Leorcham knew that Deirdre's beauty could be hidden no longer.

Conor fell in love with Deirdre and asked her to be his wife.

Deirdre said he must wait for a year. She could not refuse Conor but she loved Naoise whom she had seen in her dreams.

Conor brought Deirdre to his castle. When she saw Naoise outside the castle, she called him by name. Naoise looked to see who called and fell in love.

"She is betrothed to the king," his brothers warned.

"We will take her away from here."

Conor was jealous when he discovered that Deirdre had gone with Naoise. He sent warriors to pursue them. Deirdre and the sons of Usna fled to an island across the sea. There they lived happily till Conor discovered where they were. He sent a warrior with a message of peace.

Deirdre did not trust Conor but Naoise believed his promise. He brought Deirdre back to Ulster.

Leorcham, Deirdre's old nurse, came to see her. "Prepare to defend yourselves," she warned. "Conor is planning some treachery."

She went back to Conor and told him that Deirdre's beauty had faded but Conor did not believe her. He ordered his soldiers to kill Naoise and his brothers.

The soldiers attacked the house where they lay sleeping. All night and all next day the brothers fought against Conor's men. One by one they were overpowered till at last all three were dead.

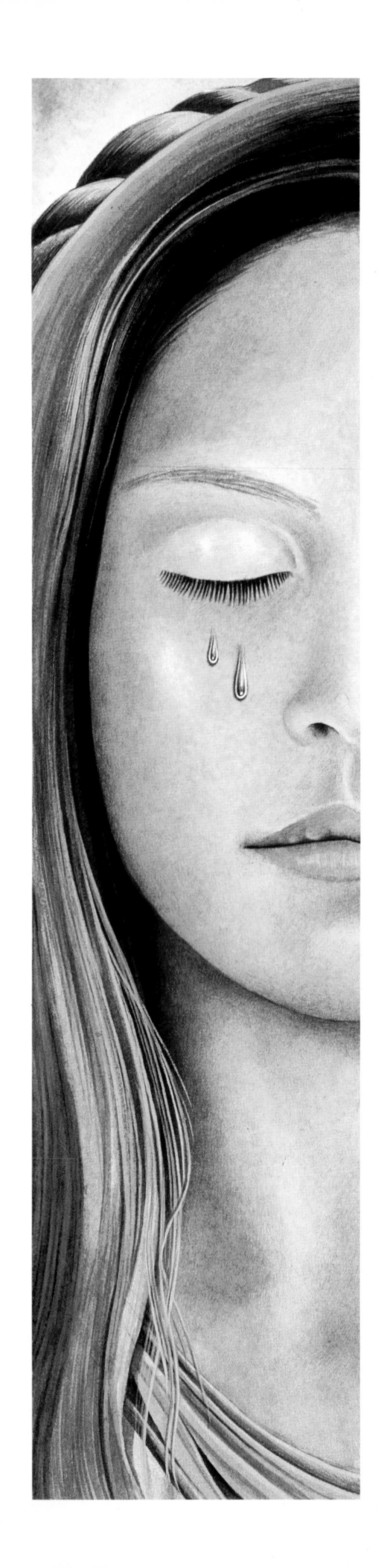

Deirdre was crazed with grief. She threw herself on Naoise's body and kissed him on the lips. Then she fled away. All night she wandered. In the morning she heard the sound of the sea and saw a carpenter carving a mast for a boat. He was using a sharp knife for his task.

"I will give you a richly jewelled ring for that knife," she said to the carpenter.

He saw her beauty and the tears in her eyes and could not refuse.

Deirdre went down to the edge of the sea. "I will not live without Naoise," she cried and drove the knife into her breast. When Conor came searching for her he found only her white body washed by the waves.

There was anger in Ulster when it became known that Conor had broken his promise. Cathbad the Druid laid a curse on Eamhain Macha, that none of the race of Conor should rule again till the end of time and so it is to this day.

Fergus Mac Leda and the Monster

Iubdan was king of the Little People of Ireland. He was proud of his kingdom. "Where are there warriors greater than mine?" he boasted.

"In Ulster the smallest man is a giant compared to your warriors," Eisirt, his bard, said. He challenged the king to go to Ulster and taste the porridge of Fergus Mac Leda, King of Ulster.

Iubdan crossed the sea to Ireland in an eggshell boat. Night was falling when he reached the king's castle. He knocked at the kitchen door and when a giant lad opened it he slipped inside unseen.

He waited till all were asleep. Then he climbed up the side of the huge porridge pot, heaved himself over the rim and fell into the porridge.

In the morning the cook found him and brought him to King Fergus. Fergus was greatly amused at the boastful little king. To punish him for his vanity he held him hostage till he gave him a gift of magic shoes, which gave to anyone who wore them the power to walk under water.

From that time forward Fergus spent his time wandering through the loughs and rivers of Ireland.

Leabharlann
Contae na Midhe
02465921

He saw strange and wonderful creatures and met the water people who live in the deep. One day, as he wandered on the bottom of a lough near his own castle, a fearsome monster attacked him. Its teeth were long and sharp like sword blades and its hide was covered with huge fishy scales.

Terrified, Fergus turned and fled before the creature. Just as it snapped at him with its terrible jaws he reached the edge of the lough and leaped to the safety of the land.

He did not venture into the lough again. He put away his magic shoes and set about attending to his kingdom.

What he did not know was that the look of terror had become fixed on his face. The queen and nobles saw that his face was awry but they did not tell him. The queen warned the servants not to speak of it and ordered them to hide all the mirrors in the castle so that the king could not see his reflection.

For a long time Fergus did not know what had happened to him. He forgot the magic shoes and the monster of the lough.

Then one day, when he was out hunting, he stooped over a well to drink. In the clear still water of the well he saw his own reflection. He saw the look of terror fixed on his face and remembered his encounter with the monster. He knew then that he must overpower the monster for his face to be restored.

Once again he put on the magic shoes which Iubdan had given him. He armed himself with his sword and spear and went to the lough. His warriors followed. They watched him walk into the lough and disappear from sight.

For three days and three nights they waited. Time and time again the water frothed and churned. On the fourth day the water turned red with blood. The monster rose roaring from the lough and sank down again.

Then the warriors saw Fergus. He rose from the water, his sword in one hand and in the other the monster's head. His face was handsome once more.

"I have won the battle," he cried out. "The monster of the lough will not trouble us again."

Cúchulainn was the greatest champion of all Ireland. When Queen Maeve of Connacht stole the Brown Bull of Cooley from Ulster, Cúchulainn made her pay dearly for it. He killed many of her champions and drove her army back to the borders of Connacht. Maeve was angry and longed for vengeance.

She sent for the three daughters of the magician Calatin. Calatin was one of the champions whom Cúchulainn had killed. His daughters were evil one-eyed witches, skilled in their father's magic arts.

"Do you wish to avenge the death of your father?" Maeve asked.

"We do," cried the three one-eyed daughters.

"Then you must go to all the countries of the world and into the underworld to learn all enchantments and charms. When you come back we will take our revenge against Cúchulainn."

The daughters of Calatin went to all the countries of the world, learning wicked charms and spells. They went down into the underworld and learned the black arts of Vulcan, the god of the underworld. Vulcan forged three spears and gave them to the daughters of Calatin. "A king will die by each of these spears," he said.

Maeve waited for a year and a day till the daughters of Calatin returned. They flew up to her window casement. "We are ready," they shrieked. "It is time."

Maeve sent at once for Cúchulainn's chief enemies, Erc, Luga and Cúroi, and gave to them the enchanted spears which the daughters of Calatin had brought from the underworld.

"Who will die by these spears?" asked Luga.

"Three kings will die by them," cried the one-eyed daughters.

Maeve sent them to use their evil spells against Cúchulainn while she prepared her army to march towards Ulster.

The daughters of Calatin flew through the sky until they came to Eamhain Macha. They filled the air with warlike sounds: the stamp of horses, the thunder of chariot wheels and the cries of wounded warriors.

When Cúchulainn heard these sounds he seized his weapons and prepared to defend Ulster. His friends saw that he was under a spell and tried to stop him going.

"These are only phantoms of the air," they said but Cúchulainn could see the smoke of burning houses and hear the wailing of women. The thistles in the fields became marching armies and leaves in the wind were troops of fighting men. His battle rage came on him and no one could hold him back.

He ordered his chariot-driver Laegh to yoke his horse, the Grey of Macha, to his chariot and they drove to meet the enemies of Ulster.

On their way they passed a young maiden weeping and wailing by a stream. She was washing a warrior's tunic and, as she washed, the water of the stream turned red as blood. Cúchulainn recognised the tunic as his own.

"Who is that maiden?" he asked.

"She is the daughter of the goddess of war," Laegh replied and they both knew that Cúchulainn would not come back from the battle alive.

When the enemies of Cúchulainn

saw him coming in his chariot, and the hero-light shining about his head, they linked their shields together. Twice Cúchulainn drove them back with his mighty sword. Twice they rallied again.

Then his enemies, Erc, Luga and Cúroi advanced, bearing the enchanted spears.

Erc was first to fling his spear. It glanced off Cúchulainn's shield and pierced his driver, Laegh, in the side.

"You said this spear would kill a king," Erc said to the daughters of Calatin.

"Laegh was the king of chariot-drivers," shrieked the one-eyed daughters.

Cúchulainn laid his faithful servant on the ground and took the chariot reins in his own hands. Then he faced his enemies once more.

Luga was next to throw his spear. It struck Cúchulainn's horse, the Grey of Macha.

"You said that spear would kill a king," Luga said to the daughters of Calatin.

"The Grey of Macha was the king of horses," the one-eyed daughters screamed.

Cúroi was last to throw his spear.

It pierced the side of Cúchulainn, the king of champions.

Mortally wounded, Cúchulainn sank to the ground. His enemies were still afraid of him and did not dare come close.

"Let me drink at the edge of the lake," he said. Maeve's warriors stood aside to let him pass and Cúchulainn went to the lake to drink. Then he stood, and tied himself with his girdle to a pillar of stone near the lakeside so that he would die standing up.

For a long time his enemies waited and even when the hero-light faded from Cúchulainn's brow they did not dare approach. Not until a raven came and perched on his shoulder did they know for certain that Cúchulainn, the greatest of champions, was dead.

The Dream of Angus

Angus was the son of the Dagda, a king of the fairy race who ruled Ireland long ago. He was handsome and young. Wherever he went, four birds flew around his head. These were his kisses which were so magical that they turned into birds and sang sweetly for all who came near.

One night Angus dreamed of a maiden more beautiful than any he had ever seen. Her long hair shimmered like gold on her shoulders and her neck was slender and white as a swan's. When Angus reached to touch her she disappeared.

Night after night she came to him. Sometimes she played on a harp to make him sleep. At other times she sang to him. When Angus awoke he could think of nothing but the maiden who came to him in his dreams. He could not eat and pined away with love for her.

His mother sent for healers and wise men. They came but they could not tell what was wrong. Then Feirgne, the wisest healer of all, came to see Angus. He saw at once what ailed the young man.

"Who is the woman for whom you are pining away?" he asked.

Angus told of the maiden who came to him in his dreams.

"We will find her for you," Feirgne promised. Messengers searched all over Ireland. At last news came that a daughter of the King of Connacht might be the maiden of his dreams. She lived with many other maidens at a lake.

Angus set off in his chariot and did not stop till he came to the lake. There he saw a crowd of beautiful maidens, each wearing a chain of silver. Among them was the maiden of his dreams. She was taller and more beautiful than the other maidens. Around her neck was a chain of gold.

Angus told her of his love.

"Before you speak of love, you must first speak to my father," she replied.

"Our daughter is under enchantment," her father said. "For one half of the year she is a maiden. For the other half she is a swan."

Angus went back to the lake. The maidens were nowhere to be seen. On the water was a crowd of white swans, each wearing a silver chain, but one with a chain of gold.

Angus called and she came to him.

"Will you love me?" he asked.

"I will love you if you will become a swan for my sake."

Immediately Angus turned himself into a swan. They spread their wings and flew away. As they flew their happiness made such sweet music that all who heard it fell asleep.

The Story of Flidias

Flidias was goddess of the forests of Ireland and of the wild animals who lived there among ancient oak trees and magic hazels. When they were injured by hunters or dogs, she tended them. "With my blessing I heal the bite of the dog and the wound of the thorn and the blow of sharpened steel," she said and immediately their wounds were healed.

The animals loved Flidias. Tuan, King of the Deer, drew her golden chariot. His does gave Flidias a share of their milk for her two daughters, Liban and Fand.

The daughters of Flidias grew up to be beautiful maidens. Liban was good and wise. She used her powers of healing to help all mortal creatures. Fand, however, did not use her powers for good. She made her dwelling in a lake deep in the forest. When men or animals came there, she lured them into the lake and they were never seen again.

One day Tuan's son, a young fawn, strayed near the lake. When his mother discovered he had disappeared, she went to Tuan. "Fand has taken your son to her dwelling under the water. We will never see him again," she said sadly.

"Flidias will help us," Tuan said and together they went to her.

"I cannot force Fand to give back your son," Flidias said, "but if you can lure her from the lake I will call your son and restore him to you."

"How can Fand be lured from the lake?" Tuan asked.

"Only the sweetest music in the world will entice Fand from her home. You must find the musician who can make that music if you wish to see your son again."

Next morning, Fionn and the men of the Fianna were out hunting near to their castle. They caught sight of Tuan, King of the Deer, standing on a near hillside. At once the hounds gave chase. Instead of fleeing from them, Tuan waited till the hounds drew near, then ran before them.

All day long men and dogs followed as Tuan led them over mountains, through forests and across wide plains. It was evening when at last they came to the lake deep in the forest. Tuan turned to face the Fianna and Fionn raised his spear to kill him.

"Do not raise your spear against me," Tuan cried out in a human voice.

Astonished to hear the deer speak, Fionn laid down his spear. "Who are you and what do you want from Fionn and the Fianna?" he asked.

"I am Tuan, King of the Deer. I was once a man and now I am a deer. I have lived many lives and will live many more because I am the one who must tell the story of Ireland when the time comes for it to be written down. I ask you for the sweetest music of the Fianna. Fand, the enchantress who lives in this lake, has taken my son. Only the sweetest music in the world can lure her from her dwelling and set my son free."

"I will play my sweetest music," said Daighre, chief bard of the Fianna. He unslung his harp and played. The shadow of evening rippled on the lake but Fand did not appear.

"I will play," said Cró Deire, chief bard of the fairies. He played the sweet fairy music which has power of enchantment over all who hear it. The breeze stirred among the trees but still Fand did not appear.

"Let me play," said Suamach, youngest bard of the Fianna, whose music was sweeter than the song of the lark in the morning.

He plucked the strings of his harp and played the sweetest music that ever was heard. Out of the depths of the lake, Fand arose. Her skin was pale like moonlight and her eyes shone green as lake water. "What is that music?" she asked but Suamach did not reply. He played on while Fand left the lake and drew close to the sound of his harp.

While Fand listened, Flidias called out to the son of Tuan. Deep in the lake he heard her voice and came running swiftly to her. Flidias led the fawn to his mother.

Suamach stopped playing on his harp then and Fand sank back into the deep water. "My son is restored to us," Tuan said to Fionn, "yet when he is grown he may die by the spears of the Fianna."

"Let you remember Fionn and the Fianna when you tell the story of Ireland to those who will write it down," said Fionn, "and I will give my pledge that the Fianna will hunt none of the family of Tuan."

"I will remember," Tuan said and so it was till the King of the Deer grew old and was born once again as a silver salmon of the river and the sea.

For Patsy, my champion
and helper in all that I do

SL

For my father and mother

FO'C

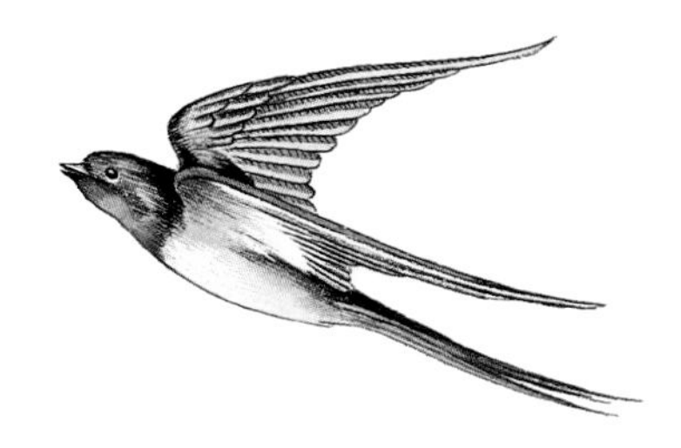

SOINBHE LALLY was born in Enniskillen in Northern Ireland. She is a playwright, short story writer and a winner of the Hennessy Award. She has written several children's books for Poolbeg including *A Hive for the Honey-Bee* (shortlisted for the Reading Association of Ireland Book Award) and *The Hungry Wind* (Bisto Merit Award). She lives in County Donegal.

FINBARR O'CONNOR was born in Cork. Since illustrating Poolbeg's *Favourite Irish Fairytales* he has illustrated four prestigious sets of stamps with An Post and numerous book covers. He lives and works in Cork.

Published 2000 by Poolbeg Press Ltd
123 Baldoyle Industrial Estate, Dublin 13, Ireland

© Soinbhe Lally 2000
Illustrations © Finbarr O'Connor 2000

The moral right of the author and illustrator has been asserted.

A catalogue record for this book is available from the British Library.

ISBN 1 85371 985 4

All rights reserved. No part of this publication may be reproduced or transmitted in any form or by any means, electronic or mechanical, including photography, recording, or any information storage or retrieval system, without permission in writing from the publisher. The book is sold subject to the condition that it shall not, by way of trade or otherwise, be lent, resold or otherwise circulated without the publisher's prior consent in any form of binding or cover other than that in which it is published and without a similar condition, including this condition, being imposed on the subsequent purchaser.

Design by Artmark
Set by Artmark in Hiroshige 14/27
Printed by Dai Nippon, Hong Kong.